The Gryphon Press

—a voice for the voiceless—

These books are dedicated to those who foster compassion toward all animals.

For my son, Daniel Prevost, who truly knows what it means to care.—J.P.

In memory of Lauren Costa (2002–2011),
who loved her dog, Brody, and life.—J.P.

To the Williams family, especially Samara and Mario,
without whom these illustrations would not have been possible,
and to Polliwog, as always.—A.H.

Text set in Berstrom by BookMobile Design and Publishing Services
Printed in Canada by Friesens Corporation

Library of Congress Control Number: 2012947075

ISBN: 978-0-940719-16-3

1 3 5 7 9 10 8 6 4 2

A portion of profits from this book will be
donated to shelters and animal rescue societies.

I am the voice of the voiceless:

Through me, the dumb shall speak;

Till the deaf world's ear be made to hear

The cry of the wordless weak.

—from a poem by Ella Wheeler Wilcox, early 20th-century poet

It's Raining Pups
and dogs!

written by
Jeanne Prevost

illustrated by
Amelia Hansen

When Lauren and her dad arrived home, they let sleepy Scout out of her crate, and she flopped down on her bed. Lauren noticed her shaved belly and the small, red cut that had been stitched closed.

"I still don't know why Scout had to have that spay operation," Lauren said to Dad. "It would be so much fun for me if she had puppies."

"Lauren, this is the way to take good care of our dog," Dad said. "No matter how much you'd like to have puppies, spaying is the right thing to do."

"But I want puppies!" Lauren cried and marched into her room.

The next morning, Scout bounced up to greet
Lauren. She held her ball and pranced.
The operation hadn't bothered Scout one bit.
But it bothered Lauren a lot.

Her chance for Scout to have puppies
was lost. She would never, ever have
her dream of raising a litter of sweet,
lovable puppies.

"Dad, I really, really, really, really wanted Scout to have puppies," Lauren said at breakfast. "I wanted to keep one! All my friends wanted one, too."

Dad said, "Let's go for a ride, honey."

They settled Scout comfortably in her crate with a chew toy and set out.

As they drove along,
Dad pointed out the
town's animal shelter.
A sign read, *We Need
Food Donations.*

A short distance away in
the neighboring town, they
passed another, larger animal
shelter. Its sign announced
an upcoming fund-raising walk
and urged folks to take part.

Lauren wondered what Dad was up to. Hope swelled like a balloon inside her heart.

"Are we going to get another dog so that we can raise puppies?" she asked.

Dad kept driving. They parked in front of an enormous building. Thunder growled, lightning flickered, and rain started pouring down.

"It's raining cats and dogs!" Lauren said.

"Maybe *pups* and dogs," said Dad.

They entered the animal shelter through its glass doors
and stood in a gleaming waiting area. A friendly receptionist came over.

"Hi. I'm Terry. Would you like to see our dogs or our cats?" she asked.

"Dogs," Dad answered.

Lauren smiled. *Dad must
be sorry he had Scout spayed.
Now we'll get a dog we won't
spay, and we'll have a litter of
puppies!* she thought.

When they entered the
kennel area, the barking was
deafening, urgent, and constant.

The hallway stretched so far ahead of them
that Lauren couldn't see the other end. Metal bars
rattled as howling, whining, yelping, and yapping dogs
jumped against them. Some dogs cowered in their corners.
Some stood and stared.

Volunteers and shelter employees moved through the area with leashes,
water bowls, food, and cleaning tools.

"How many dogs do you have here?" Dad asked, raising his voice over the din.

Taz, Finn
& Ruby
lab mix

"Adoptable ones? We have 114," Terry shouted back. "But the actual population we have today is 118."

Lauren frowned. "What do you mean?" she asked.

Terry looked at Dad. He nodded.

Terry said, "At times we get a dog that has had too hard a life to make a good pet." Her voice trailed off. "We can't find homes for those dogs."

"Is it always this full?" Dad asked.

"Always," Terry said.

Lauren wandered the aisles.
She read the tags on the doors.

These dogs need homes, she thought. How will they all get adopted?
I wish I could help.

I'm glad Scout lives with us and not here.

"Do you want a puppy, or a grown dog, or a certain breed?" Terry asked Lauren.

"I wanted *my* dog to have puppies,"
Lauren admitted.

"Most people come here looking for a
puppy," Terry explained. "But look at this
guy over here. He's so sweet and so loving.
He shouldn't get passed up for a younger dog."

Lauren noticed the gentle wisdom in the
older dog's eyes.

"Um . . . I actually came here
to . . . um . . . volunteer . . .
to help homeless dogs,"
Lauren told Terry.

Terry smiled and guided Lauren to a dog nearby. She showed Lauren where the leashes were kept and how to safely take the animal out of its kennel. Then Lauren led a terrier, frolicking for joy, into the play area for a romp.

Afterward, Lauren signed up to play with homeless dogs for one hour a week.

Stepping outside into sunshine after being in the shelter felt like waking from a dream. Yet Lauren's mind flashed images of lonely animals pawing at metal bars.

"What happens to the dogs who don't find homes?" Lauren asked. "Do they live at the shelter all their lives?"

"All their *short* lives," Dad answered.

On the drive home, Dad quietly said, "There are more dogs in the world than there are people who will take care of them."

Lauren said, "If Scout had puppies, we'd give them to our friends. We wouldn't ever drop them at a shelter."

"But every single puppy you give to a friend or sell to someone means one less home for a shelter dog."

Lauren was quiet the rest of the way, thinking of the dogs she had just seen, dogs who might never find homes. And there were more dogs at the other shelters they had passed, all waiting for someone to rescue them.

At home, Lauren let Scout out of her crate. She threw Scout's ball, and Scout skidded across the floor and pounced on it.

"I'm glad you had that spay operation," Lauren whispered. "No matter how much I'd like you to have puppies, spaying is the right thing, okay? It's the way to take good care of you.

And remember, I'll *always* take good care of you."

Also Available from The Gryphon Press

Always Blue for Chicu

ISBN: 978-0-940719-09-5 / Text and Illustration by Karen Dugan / $16.95 / Jacketed Cloth / 32 Pages / Ages 5 and Up / Recommended—The National Humane Education Society / Independent Publishers Bronze Medal

"This heartwarming and delightful story will intrigue and interest children while it charms their parents. It is a pleasure to see a children's picture book that is exciting and amazing yet accessible and accurate. *Always Blue for Chicu* captures the life and spirit of this fascinating parrot and the saga of his finding a home with people who understand his needs." —Joanna Burger, author of *The Parrot Who Owns Me*

Are You Ready for Me?

ISBN: 978-0-940719-08-8 / Text by Claire Buchwald / Illustration by Amelia Hansen / $6.95 / Paperback with Flaps / 24 Pages / Ages 5 and Up / Recommended—The National Humane Education Society

"A guide to responsible care, and inspiring compassion and understanding, this book will benefit all young readers— and all dogs." —Dr. Michael W. Fox, veterinarian, syndicated columnist, and author of numerous dog books

At the Dog Park with Sam and Lucy

eBook ISBN: 978-0-940719-18-7 / Text by Daisy Bix / Illustration by Amelia Hansen / $15.00 / 24 Pages / Ages 5 and Up

Sam and Lucy are excited to be going to the dog park with their "people." Written entirely in short phrases "spoken" by the various animals, the text is breezy and light, switching quickly from one pup to another. The crisp watercolor illustrations capture their energy and exuberance. The many breeds depicted are listed on the inside flap of the book jacket, encouraging readers to find them in the pictures. —*School Library Journal*

Buddy Unchained

ISBN: 978-0-940719-01-9 / Text by Daisy Bix / Illustration by Joe Hyatt / $15.95 / Jacketed Cloth / 24 Pages / Ages 5 and Up / ASPCA Henry Bergh Children's Book Award Winner / Humane Society of the United States Youth KIND Children's Book Award Winner / Recommended—The National Humane Education Society

"*Buddy Unchained* is a deeply moving look at a dog abandoned and adopted. The story is simple yet of vast importance, and at the end we want nothing more than to make sure that all the Buddys of the world are loved and cared for like this patient, easy-to-please pup." —Janet Leimeister, Events Manager, The Capitola Book Store

Call the Horse Lucky

ISBN: 978-0-940719-10-1 / Text by Juanita Havill / Illustration by Nancy Lane / $16.95 / Jacketed Cloth / 24 Pages / Ages 5 and Up

"*Call the Horse Lucky* is a gift to all readers. As an equine veterinarian for many years and dedicated to teaching correct animal husbandry I applaud this book. The story, the husbandry discussed, the solutions to a problem, the economic values and the information in the epilogue are all really correct and to the point in my opinion. The illustrations/paintings are an additional gift and I felt as if the people were all someone I had met in my practice." —Pat Frederick, Doctor of Veterinary Medicine

A Home for Dakota

ISBN: 978-0-940719-05-7 / Text by Jan Zita Grover / Illustration by Nancy Lane / $16.95 / Jacketed Cloth / 24 Pages / Ages 5 and Up / Humane Society Youth KIND Children's Book Award Winner / ASPCA Henry Bergh Children's Honor Book / Recommended—The National Humane Education Society

"*A Home for Dakota* is a poignant story of hope. The text and outstanding illustrations will help build understanding, empathy, and compassion in young readers toward both dogs and other children. This book is a must-read in elementary school classrooms and will be the springboard for valuable discussions and research. Highly recommended." —Sheila Schwartz, EdD, Chairperson, United Federation of Teachers, Humane Education Committee, NYC

It's Raining Cats and Cats!

ISBN: 978-0-940719-06-4 / Text by Jeanne Prevost / Illustration by Amelia Hansen / $15.95 / Jacketed Cloth / 24 Pages / Ages 5 and Up / ASPCA Henry Bergh Children's Book Award Winner / Humane Society of the United States Youth KIND Children's Honor Book / Recommended—The National Humane Education Society

"*It's Raining Cats and Cats!* offers a lighthearted look at the serious problem that overpopulation plays in creating homeless animals. This beautifully illustrated and thought-provoking story shows why providing proper care and finding good homes for a growing houseful of cats would be very challenging." —Kathleen Makolinski, Doctor of Veterinary Medicine, Director of Veterinary Outreach, ASPCA

KokoCat, Inside and Out

ISBN: 978-0-940719-12-5 / Text by Lynda Graham-Barber / Illustration by Nancy Lane / $16.95 / Jacketed Cloth / 24 Pages / Ages 5 and Up / eBook ISBN: 978-0-940719-15-6 / $15.00 / Moonbeam Children's Book Award, Silver Medal

KokoCat, a well-loved house cat, takes advantage of an open door and runs away to explore.

"*KokoCat, Inside and Out* gets across an important message without 'preaching,' in a manner that will appeal to all ages of cat lovers as well as to the uninitiated. An important book with a vital point!" —Libby Phillips Meggs, author of *Go Home! The True Story of James the Cat*

Maggie's Second Chance

ISBN: 978-0-940719-11-8 / Text by Nancy Furstinger / Illustration by Joe Hyatt / $16.95 / Jacketed Cloth / 24 Pages / Ages 5 and Up / Moonbeam Children's Book Award, Gold Medal, Spirit Award

"*Maggie's Second Chance* is the touching, and all-too-common, story of a dog abandoned when a family moves and heartlessly leaves her behind. The illustrations are lovingly and beautifully done, as is the prose. Based on a true story, this book is a great springboard for teaching lessons of compassion to students." —Pamela Kramer, *National Examiner*

Max Talks to Me

ISBN: 978-0-940719-03-3 / Text by Claire Buchwald / Illustration by Karen Ritz / $16.95 / Jacketed Cloth / 24 Pages / Ages 5 and Up / Humane Society of the United States Youth KIND Children's Honor Book / Recommended—The National Humane Education Society

"In *Max Talks to Me,* Claire Buchwald brilliantly shares a story of love and devotion between a child and his beloved furry friend and the caring behaviors that allow such a rich relationship to develop. This heartwarming account will make a fine addition to my grandson's (and any child's) bookshelf!" —Bonnie Jean Flom, educational consultant, former elementary school principal

Ms. April & Ms. Mae: A Fable

ISBN: 978-0-940719-07-1 / Text and Illustration by Karen Dugan / $17.95 / Jacketed Cloth / 40 Pages / Ages 5 and Up / Forward Reviews Book of the Year Award Finalist, Children's Picture Book Category

"This is just the book Mother Nature would order. The author clearly understands the role that our children will play in the future health of our planet. I invite the reader to apply Ms. Mae's persistence and wit to saving some elbow room for all kinds of wildlife and habitats." —Nancy Gibson, Cofounder, International Wolf Center, and author of *Wolves*

For Parents and Other Adults

Sadly, there are far more dogs than there are homes to care for them. According to 2009 estimates by the Humane Society of the United States, six to eight *million* dogs are abandoned or turned in to shelters every year in our country. Only half of these shelter dogs are eventually adopted. The other three to four million dogs are destroyed. Every year.

The most important step we as individuals can take to stop the killing of innocent dogs is to promote spay/neuter programs. Spaying/neutering lowers the number of dogs who are euthanized. Many animal organizations sponsor spay/neuter clinics. In most areas you can find a high-quality, low-cost spay/neuter clinic by calling your local animal humane society. The veterinary costs associated with pregnancy, delivery, and puppy food are much greater than those of sterilization surgery.

A vital part of improving the lot of homeless dogs is to adopt from a shelter when you add a dog to your family. If your heart is set on a purebred dog, consider breed rescue organizations. Each breed has a rescue group you can check out online.

While reputable purebred dog breeders do their best to find appropriate homes for the puppies in every litter, in many areas of the country, large breeding facilities (called puppy mills), whose concern is only profit, keep dogs in small, dirty cages where females give birth to litter after litter without ever getting proper care, love, or companionship. When the females are too old to produce litters, they are killed.

Puppy mills provide most of the puppies for pet shops. In addition, many puppies or dogs sold through ads on the Internet are sick or ill-cared for and originate from a puppy mill. Humane groups suggest never buying a puppy from a pet store or through an ad on the Internet from a breeder whose facilities *you have not personally visited*. It's easy to be swindled by an unscrupulous dealer and receive a pet with lifelong health problems. Buying from such a dealer will promote more breeding cycles for the maltreated mother dogs and add to the problem of overpopulation.

In addition to reducing overbreeding and euthanasia, spaying/neutering provides other benefits to your dog. A neutered male dog will be calmer, less aggressive, and protected from testicular cancer. He will not roam the neighborhood in search of mates. A spayed female dog will be healthier and more content, protected not only from pregnancy but also from uterine or ovarian cancer. She will not go into heat, bleed, or attract male dogs.

Additional resources include:

Bland, Alastair. "Man's Best Friend or the World's Number-One Pest?" July 18, 2012. www.smithsonianmag.com

Duchovny, David. www.600million.org

"The Shelter Population Index Study." National Council on Pet Population Study and Policy. www.petpopulation.org

"Puppy Mills." www.aspca.org

"The Facts about Pet Overpopulation." http://animalkind.org

Zelman, Joanna. "Animal Overpopulation: What's the Solution to 600 Million Stray Dogs?" May 18, 2011. www.huffingtonpost.com